The Playground Snake

First published in 2002 by
Franklin Watts
96 Leonard Street
London
EC2A 4XD

Franklin Watts Australia
56 O'Riordan Street
Alexandria
NSW 2015

Text © Brian Moses 2002
Illustration © David Mostyn 2002

A CIP catalogue record for this book is available
from the British Library.

ISBN 0 7496 4699 3 (hbk)
ISBN 0 7496 4706 X (pbk)

Series Editor: Jackie Hamley
Series Advisor: Dr Barrie Wade
Cover Design: Jason Anscomb
Design: Peter Scoulding

Printed in Hong Kong

The
Playground
Snake

by Brian Moses and David Mostyn

W
FRANKLIN WATTS
LONDON • SYDNEY

The snake in the school
playground was fed up.

Once, long ago, the children used to play with him. But now they hardly even noticed him.

They jumped and stamped on him
and ran across his tail. They didn't
want him in their games at all.

The snake in the playground had a terrible headache.

He had tail ache and tummy ache.

"That's it," thought the snake.

"I've put up with too much of this!"

And he decided to go and find

some friends to play with.

At the end of playtime, nobody saw the slippery snake slithering across the playground.

The children didn't see the slippery snake slide silently through the door behind them.

The children in the corridor didn't see the snake as they walked quietly to the gym.

The head teacher didn't see the
snake when she climbed the stairs
to her office.

The children in the gym didn't see the snake as they hung from the ropes and bars.

14

The teachers didn't see the snake when they sipped their coffees in the staff room.

The school cook didn't see the
snake as he tasted the spaghetti.

Even the school caretaker didn't
see the snake as he swept the
floor in the changing room.

18

But everyone in Class 3 saw the snake, trying to hide in their wormery.

They said that he could stay there and they painted pictures of him.

He had a part in their class play.

And he was brilliant at
snakes and ladders!

The snake was delighted to have so
many friends. Everyone was happy.

Then, one day, the head
teacher saw the snake.

"A classroom is no place for a snake, he'll have to go!" she ordered.

"Don't worry, children," said their teacher. "I know just the place for a snake. I know how we can make him happy."

And the very next day...

The children found a sunny corner
in the playground.

They painted and they planted until they'd given the snake his very own rainforest.

And he liked it so much, he decided to stay!

And now he doesn't mind when
the children jump and stamp
on him...

...as long as he is part
of the game!

Hopscotch has been specially designed to fit the requirements of the National Literacy Strategy. It offers real books by top authors and illustrators for children developing their reading skills.

There are 12 Hopscotch stories to choose from:

Marvin, the Blue Pig
Written by Karen Wallace, illustrated by Lisa Williams

0 7496 4473 7 (hbk)
0 7496 4619 5 (pbk)

Plip and Plop
Written by Penny Dolan, illustrated by Lisa Smith

0 7496 4474 5 (hbk)
0 7496 4620 9 (pbk)

The Queen's Dragon
Written by Anne Cassidy, illustrated by Gwyneth Williamson

0 7496 4472 9 (hbk)
0 7496 4618 7 (pbk)

Flora McQuack
Written by Penny Dolan, illustrated by Kay Widdowson

0 7496 4475 3 (hbk)
0 7496 4621 7 (pbk)

Willie the Whale
Written by Joy Oades, illustrated by Barbara Vagnozzi

0 7496 4477 X (hbk)
0 7496 4623 3 (pbk)

Naughty Nancy
Written by Anne Cassidy, illustrated by Desideria Guicciardini

0 7496 4476 1 (hbk)
0 7496 4622 5 (pbk)

Run!
Written by Sue Ferraby, illustrated by Fabiano Fiorin

0 7496 4698 5 (hbk)
0 7496 4705 1 (pbk)

The Playground Snake
Written by Brian Moses, illustrated by David Mostyn

0 7496 4699 3 (hbk)
0 7496 4706 X (pbk)

"Sausages!"
Written by Anne Adeney, illustrated by Roger Fereday

0 7496 4700 0 (hbk)
0 7496 4707 8 (pbk)

The Truth about Hansel and Gretel
Written by Karina Law, illustrated by Elke Counsell

0 7496 4701 9 (hbk)
0 7496 4708 6 (pbk)

Pippin's Big Jump
Written by Hilary Robinson, illustrated by Sarah Warburton

0 7496 4703 5 (hbk)
0 7496 4710 8 (pbk)

Whose Birthday Is It?
Written by Sherryl Clark, illustrated by Jan Smith

0 7496 4702 7 (hbk)
0 7496 4709 4 (pbk)